E Ber

The Berenstain Bears VISIT UNCLE TEX

Stan & Jan Berenstain

Reader's Digest **Kids**

Westport, Connecticut

Come. It's time to leave
for our ranch vacation.

But, Papa, this isn't the way
to the train station.

We cannot visit Tex
by train.
His ranch is far.
We'll go by plane.

Wow! Wait 'til we tell
Cousin Fred.
Look! There's the airport
just ahead!

Fasten your seat belts.
We're ready to fly.

We're above the clouds!
We're high in the sky!

Look! Rivers and forests
down below!
On the mountaintops,
caps of snow!

Wake up! Wake up,
Papa Bear!
The pilot says
we're almost there.

PLEASE STAY IN YOUR SEATS
DO NOT STAND
WE ARE JUST
ABOUT TO LAND

There's Uncle Tex
right over there.
As you can see,
he's a cowboy bear.

Just take a look
at how he's dressed:
in a ten-gallon hat,
chaps and vest,
cowboy boots,
and all the rest.

Welcome, folks,
to the glorious West!

Well, here's my ranch,

the B-Bar-X.

It looks great,

Uncle Tex!

We've got horses,

cattle,

a barn, of course.

This is Red,
my favorite horse.

May we ride him?

Hmm, that might be risky.
Red can be
a little frisky.

Cubs, I have ponies
for you to ride.
But first, meet Aunt Min,
my lovely bride.

Tex, I think I
can handle Red.

Red is frisky,
as I said.
But be my guest.
You go to it.

Will you please
relax, my dear?
There is not
a thing to fear.

And may I please
remind you all,
No horse on earth
can make me fall.

You must be a little
out of practice.
Er, sorry about
that giant cactus.

Your ponies, cubs.
Climb on, Sister. You, too, lad.

And here's a buggy
for your mom and dad.

This way, folks.
Follow me.
The glorious West
has lots to see.

Canyons,

cliffs,

rivers,

ridges,

the Painted Desert,

natural bridges.

Now, think of the things
that are no longer here,
the hopes and dreams
of yesteryear.

And if you use
your mind's eye,
you can almost see them
in the sky . . .

Pony Express riders
brave and bold,

folks who came West
to pan for gold,

great bison herds

and wagon trains

reached across

the western plains.

Folks, I do not like
to break the spell,
but I think I smell
a special smell.

Mmm! Mmm!
Yes, it's true!
I smell Aunt Min's
barbecue!

So back they went
to the B-Bar-X,
the home of Aunt Min
and Uncle Tex.

They rode.

They roped.

They danced.

They sang.

They came a-running

when the dinner gong rang.

They watched the lovely
sunset sky.

They listened to
the coyote's cry.

HOOOWWL

Then it was time to leave
the B-Bar-X,

to say good-bye

to Min and Tex.

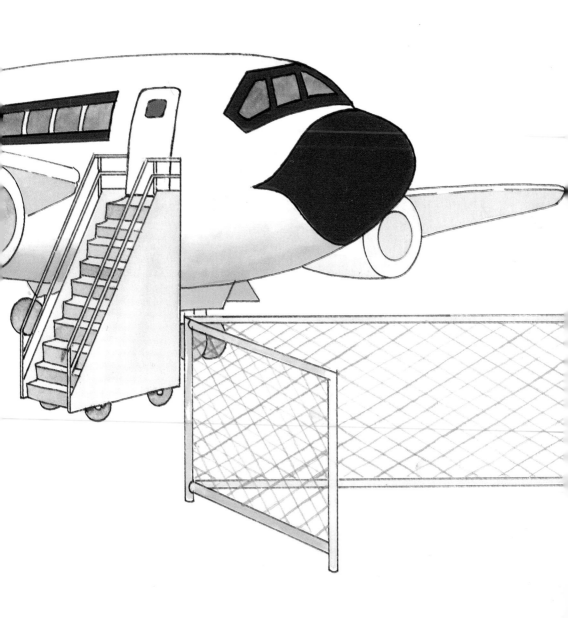

There were bear hugs

and kisses all around.

Then they were up and away . . .

and homeward bound.